The apple blossom

Here comes spring

and summer and autumn and winter

Mary Murphy

Here comes spring!

flies in the breeze.

We do some work
in the garden.

I meet my
friend in
the park.

In summer we have picnics.

The sun is high in the sky.

We rest in the shade.

The apples are ripe

and ready to pick.

Yip!

In autumn
we jump
in hills
of crunchy
leaves.

The wind messes
up the garden.

In winter the birds are hungry.

We have a snow fight.

Look at our snowdog!

Night
comes
early.

To my mother, Anna Murphy

www.dk.com

First published in Great Britain in 1999 by Dorling Kindersley Limited,
9 Henrietta Street, London WC2E 8PS
Paperback edition published in 2000

2 4 6 8 10 9 7 5 3 1

A CIP catalogue record for this book is available from the British Library.

ISBN 0-7513-7164-5 (Hardback)
ISBN 0-7513-3127-9 (Paperback)

Colour Reproduction by DOT Gradations
Printed in Hong Kong by Wing King Tong Co Ltd